K THE

VIKING

...shame
...wn...

EITH BRUMPTON

ORCHARD BOOKS

OTHER BOOKS BY KEITH BRUMPTON

Dinosaur World Cup
A Dinosaur's Book of Dinosaurs
Ig and Tig's Trip to Earth
The Mystery of the Missing Moggie
The Mystery of the Dog with 1000 Disguises
The Mystery of the Great Sheepdog Swindle
The Mystery of the Dachshund Diamonds

• DEREK BOOKS •

Who'd be a Viking?
The Creature from the Black Lagoon
Kidnapped by Ice Maidens

(All of these books are very exciting and good value—
much cheaper than a luxury cruise or a new
sports car).

To find out more about Keith Brumpton's books,
visit his website at:
http://www.okukbooks.com/kbrumpton/

Contents

READER'S CHARTER

Dear Reader,

We are glad you have chosen this book, and hope it will provide many hours of trouble-free use. The story has been written in English in order to make it easier to understand, and printed on white paper, ideal for low-light conditions.

In the unlikely event of this book not proving satisfactory, please return it, together with the original wrapping paper and a cheque for ninety pounds to—:

Christina Ssschammofanöffa,
Customer Complaints Unit,
Door Two, Table twelve,
The Corridor,
Hamely-Under-Haddock HP50S.

ORCHARD BOOKS
96 Leonard Street, London EC2A 4RH
Orchard Books Australia
14 Mars Road, Lane Cove, NSW 2066
First published in Great Britain 1998
First paperback publication 1999
Copyright © Keith Brumpton 1998
The right of Keith Brumpton to be identified as the Author and
Illustrator of this Work has been asserted by him in accordance
with the Copyright, Designs and Patents Act, 1988.
A CIP catalogue record for this book is available from the
British Library.
1 86039 359 4 (hardback)
1 86039 603 8 (paperback)
Printed in Great Britain

Chapter One: Chief Harald's mini-break.

It was the month of Thor-gust. Birds were twittering, contented mooses were chomping on fresh summer clover, and the Vikings of Upper Elkshead were preparing for life without their chief, Harald Hafnomörssy.

Did you pack my spear, sweetheart?

Yes, it's with your chess-set and copy of the Axe-Files. *

travelling spear

holiday dagger

trunks

Mrs. Chief

* Popular Viking series.

Every year at the same time, Chief Harald took his summer vacation, heading for the popular resort of Bloodpool where he rented a cottage.

Bloodpool was famous for its illuminations...

Saxon village on fire

Monastery alight

Rampaging Warriors with torches

"Oh, I can't wait," he burbled enthusiastically.

It's fun to slay, but nice to get away.

"...Hunting elk... Chopping logs... Shield surfing..."

"You've earned it," said the Chief's wife, Hedda (or 'Good Hedda', as she was sometimes known). "I think you've done more killing and pillaging than ever this year. It's time to put your feet up."

The Chief wore a proud smile. "It *has* been a good year," he growled. "I just hope there'll be a few monks left to attack when I get back."

(The Vikings loved to attack monasteries. They were full of riches, were poorly defended, and there was free parking.)

Whenever the Chief went on holiday, the Viking Council met to choose a temporary successor – someone who would look after things while the Chief was away.

The Council was due to meet that very evening, and Derek the Depressed Viking wasn't looking forward to it.

← Derek's invite

"I always get put next to Olaf Dednafffellur and his sweaty armpits. I defy anyone to enjoy their supper with him around. And he keeps flicking bits of moss into my soup."

"Why don't you behead him?" suggested Derek's mum, who was as hard as a polar bear's toe-nails and twice as sharp.

Derek shook his head.

"No point in annoying people."

"You're a Viking, son... It's your *job* to annoy people. Now, isn't it time you went along to that meeting? And brush your beard...the Princess Anka might be there."*

Derek blushed but felt slightly less depressed.

"I shouldn't be late back unless the meat at the banquet is very tough and gristly."

* Princess Anka – Derek's intended. (He intended to kiss her one day.)

Chapter Two: Council of War.

Derek never liked Councils of War. Everyone there always looked too fierce (except for Princess Anka, of course).

He didn't think he'd ever seen so many scars, broken noses, bulging biceps and bone-cracking brawn in his life. And that was just the girls serving the wine.

Just as he feared, Derek was given a seat next to his sworn enemy, Olaf Dednafffellur, he of the sweaty armpits.

"If you see a mouse, don't faint, Deggsie," he sneered.

You can jump up onto my chair, Ha-Ha-Ha-Ha!

← Olaf

Next to Olaf was Sven Forkbeard, the favourite to take over from Chief Harald because he was, well, the fiercest warrior, and his sword always seemed that bit longer and sharper than anyone else's.

Derek thought Sven was smiling at him and waved back, but Sven was trying to get at a piece of rabbit skin which had stuck between his teeth.

Sven ↗

The Princess threw Derek a much nicer look. It was a good job he was already sitting down because his knees went weak, like a particularly tired hamster with a touch of flu!

The Chief banged his axe down on the table to bring the meeting to order. No wonder the table was in such poor shape.

"Ladies and Roughmen, welcome to the council of War. Tonight we meet to decide who will be in charge, while I, Chief Harald, take my summer holidays. We need a warrior who is like me...tall, strong and handsome..."

"...Someone who commands the respect of every warrior, and who can lead you in battle should the need arise."

Derek looked across at Sven Forkbeard. There was no doubt he would make a good choice. Derek was just about to put his hand up when he noticed Olaf Dednafffellur had already raised his own.

Probably going to suggest himself, thought Derek, trying not to breathe in through his nostrils.

The Chief saw Olaf's arm aloft and indicated that he should speak.

Derek suddenly felt hot. As if he was wearing his helmet on a sunny day. For one awful moment he thought Olaf had suggested HE, Derek, took over as chief. Then he saw the Chief nodding and chuckling to himself.

"Derek Drodnodrott... Yes... He who went to the Black Lagoon...* Yes... He's certainly tall enough... And strong... Well, two out of three isn't bad... Derek, where is Derek the Depressed?"

* See: 'The Creature from the Black Lagoon'

Derek was on his feet, but wobbling about like a new-born moose. He swallowed hard and felt one or two people slap him on the back.

The Chief asked if he would like the job.

"Aye! Three times, aye. He accepts without hesitation!" beamed the Chief. "I like that!"

And so it was that Derek came to be appointed temporary chief. Olaf Dednafffellur was the first to shake his hand, an evil gleam in his eye.

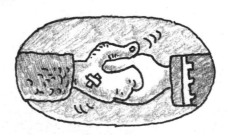

The Princess Anka bit her lip uneasily.

The Chief handed Derek his royal crown, and shook his hand so firmly it turned white.

"Run a tight ship, my boy. I'll be back in seven days to see how you've done. My loyal adviser, the Venerable Terry, is here to give you any advice you might need."

Derek looked down and saw a short, beady eyed man with a heavy wheeze. "The Venerable Terry, your loyal adviser, Master."

Derek didn't like the look of him and wished his friend Frank the seagull was around. It seemed he was off on his holidays too.

Meanwhile, in a dark corner...

Chapter Three: Enough to make a Crowned Man cry.

The crown, it had to be said, was a good fit. And quite comfortable. Unfortunately, the throne was a bit tight, Derek being much larger than Chief Harald.

Derek's mum was as proud as a monk with a new writing set.

"I wish your dad could have been around to see this."

Well why didn't you wake him up?

Princess Anka had just returned from seeing her father off.

"Don't worry, Derek, I'm sure everything will be OK. But don't trust *anyone*. Especially not the Venerable Terry... Wear your sword at all times, and never walk down dark alley-ways alone. And don't leave your back unguarded!

"I'm always here if you need someone to talk to. What happened to that little seagull of yours?" she asked.

Good question!

Chapter Four: Chief's Hut.

It was the dead of night and Derek was ready for bed. Although in the past he'd often been 'ready for bed', he'd never actually slept in one, because his mother said it would 'turn him into a softy'. The nearest he'd ever got was one birthday when the goats had given him a corner of their hay.

Now he was a chief, however, things would be different. The Venerable Terry showed him into the hut where he would be kipping, and gave a quick guided tour...

"This is where your weapons are stored. And a choice of shields in here... And there...the royal bed..."

red splodge

"It looks great," beamed Derek.

"Yes," continued the Venerable Terry, a strange whining tone in his voice, "you should sleep well...this is a famous bed. It's the same one in which Erik the Beige was killed on his wedding night, and that's the stain from Karl Bluntsword who was slain where he'd lain..."

Slain where he'd lain? The red stain?!?

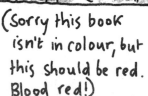

(Sorry this book isn't in colour, but this should be red. Blood red!)

Derek went white as a seagull's wing.

But worry not, my lord, nine out of every ten attempts to kill Viking chiefs end in failure.

"Nine out of ten? How often does this sort of thing go on?"

"Goodnight, my lord," wheezed the Venerable Terry. "Sleep tight."

Derek tossed and turned like a restless omelette.

"What if someone tries to kill *me*?" He tried going to sleep with his chain-mail on, and then with a shield on top of the sheets, but it was too hot.

"I need a glass of water."

The wind was howling like a pack of angry wolves. (Or an angry pack of wolves was howling like the wind, who knows...)

Every rustle or creak or tap of rain made Derek more afraid.

"But I really do need a drink of water."

He got up and stumbled in the darkness across to where the drinking jugs were stored.

"I'd better take a sip at a time in case it's poisoned."

Derek crept back to his bed, and then froze in horror. In the middle of the mattress, where he'd been sleeping, was a large sword. It was sticking right through the sheets, more or less where Derek's chest would have been!

He felt depressed. It was going to be a long night, and one thing was certain - sweet dreams were not going to feature!

Chapter Five: Rise and Whine.

extra chain-mail under-wear.

Derek woke, sunshine streaming in his face.
He checked to see he was still alive, and to
his amazement found he was. Still weary
from the restless night, he rose slowly and
began to get dressed.

Now I've survived that, maybe being
chief won't be so bad, he thought, wondering
if his new position entitled him to extra
portions of 'Moose-li'* at breakfast.

* Popular Viking breakfast cereal.

Before he could finish trimming his beard, the Venerable Terry had appeared in his hut, accompanied by Olaf Dednafffellur. They seemed surprised to see Derek.

"Er, good morning, Derek... Er, Chief."

"Good morning, Olaf."

"Good morning, Chief."

"Good morning, Venerable Terry. I was just going to have breakfast."

"All in good time, your majesty. But first you must have a meeting with your council of advisers."

"We're already in," snarled Olaf. "*We're* your advisers, and we've got lots of good advice."

Derek didn't like the sound of this at all. If he wanted advice, he'd rather have asked Frank or the Princess Anka, not the shifty twosome who stood before him now.

"We thought you could start the day just like Chief Harald," suggested Olaf, innocently. "Stick to the same routine and everyone will be happy."

Derek thought this sounded quite reasonable. He imagined Chief Harald beginning the day with a very large breakfast indeed, then perhaps a little walk by the seashore, then a little nap...

"So how does Chief Harald start the day?"

"Bear wrestling," replied the Venerable Terry, trying to keep a straight face. "The Chief always liked to remind everyone of his great strength by going a few rounds with a local grizzly."

"We've got a small one for you to start with."

The colour was draining fast from Derek's cheeks.

"The whole village is outside, waiting to see how you get on."

It was true. Derek opened the door of his new hut to find a large crowd assembled, and a small area of grass roped off. In one corner sat a large and unfriendly looking bear.

Olaf explained that the Chief would normally go up to the bear, throw it over his shoulder a couple of times, give it a couple of bear hugs and stroll off for breakfast.

Derek had never wrestled a bear before and he didn't fancy starting now, but maybe if he shoved the grizzly a couple of times, that might keep everyone happy...

Things were beginning to look pretty grim when, quite by accident, Derek discovered that his opponent was ticklish. The giant bear relaxed its grip on Derek every time it got tickled. And so the wrestling match became more of a tickling contest, except that to the watching crowd it looked as if Derek had totally tamed the giant beast.

The contest ended with a bit of light-hearted rough and tumble at the end of which Derek gave the bear a slap on the back

and watched it amble off into the forest. The Villagers cheered. All except for Olaf and the Venerable Terry. Princess Anka ran up to Derek and embraced him.

Not another bear-hug, please!

"I always knew you'd make a good chief," she smiled. "Almost as good as Daddy. Only six more days to go... Take care!"

For once, it was Derek who felt cheerful and Olaf who felt depressed.

The new chief spent the rest of the day feasting and sleeping and throwing pebbles into the sea.

Chapter Six: Derek Comes Clean.

Derek woke, checked his head to see that it was still attached to the rest of his body, then opened his eyes. The first thing he saw was the Venerable Terry, polishing his crown.

"Good morning, Chief Derek. Thought I'd give your crown a quick polish. It's one of my duties you know."

Derek wondered what horrible advice his shifty adviser was going to offer today. It was bound to be depressing. So Derek decided to take matters into his own hands.

"As acting chief of Upper Elkshead, I've got a suggestion... I mean a command..."

The Venerable Terry raised one eyebrow, but made no protest, so Derek continued.

"The village has been looking really scruffy, so I thought we could have a tidy-up campaign, beginning today. Today we pick up litter! If you think that's a good idea?"

Derek's adviser stood for a long moment, his head bent to one side. He looked like a penguin with a crick in its neck, but at long last he spoke, in his usual wheezing tones...

"A s-s-splendid idea, Chief. May I make a teensy-weensy suggestion?"

early morning hair

Of course...If it doesn't involve fighting with bears.

"Why not have some villagers collect litter while the rest go off into the woods and do some tidying up there too. Let's think of the countryside as well as the village."

Derek was most impressed. For once, the Venerable Terry had come up with an idea which he liked. Derek told his wheezing second-in-command to organise the village as they'd discussed, and to begin Operation Clean-Up as soon as possible.

At last things are going my way, he thought, before cutting himself while shaving.

Olaf Dednafffellur laughed and clapped his hands together when he heard about the scheme for collecting litter.

"This is perfect!" he dribbled. "Not only will half the village be bent double gathering litter, the other half will be scattered in the forest, miles away. The perfect time for an ambush."

The Venerable Terry nodded.

"I'll contact the Berks of Berka* and tell them to attack at once. You, Olaf, must destroy the beacons by the harbour. That way Derek won't be able to signal for help from his litter-picking troops in the forest."

* Bitter enemies of the Upper Elkshead Vikings.

The two traitors tittered to themselves then went their own separate ways. Things looked bad for Derek.

Princess Anka cast her ice-blue eyes in Derek's direction.

"Are you sure this is a good idea, Deggsie? I'm all for keeping the village tidy, but..."

Derek told her not to worry and that all the litter would be stored by the Old-Rock-which-was-Struck-by-Lightning. (A local landmark. It was an old rock which...well, you can guess the rest.)

In Viking times, no one knew very much about looking after the environment. There was a bit of complaining when Derek's plan was revealed.

"Yeah, we should be doing something useful like burning a monastery or stealing gold from the Saxons."

Three hours later, half the village was in the forest, working under Sven Forkbeard's direction, while the other half remained with Derek. And they were still complaining.

A large black cloud passed across the sun, making the sky grow suddenly dark. From the harbour there sounded an unfamiliar horn call.

Moments later, a pointy arrow sailed through the air and narrowly missed Derek's left ear. The Village of Upper Elkshead was under attack.

"It's the Berks! They've landed at the harbour!"

shouted Derek, resisting the temptation to go and hide under his new bed. "Forget the litter and, er, form a fighting circle."

The bad news soon reached him that the beacons had been sabotaged. There was now no way of getting help from the Vikings in the forest... Derek was heavily outnumbered

and most of his best warriors were with
Sven. He needed a brainwave and he needed
it fast. A piece of litter blew past his foot.

"No... I mean a torch... A flame... We've got to light the litter..."

Derek, trembling, held a torch to the pile of rubbish. The wind seemed too strong for it to light, but at the last moment there was a flicker and a crackle... Flames reached into the sky and smoke began to drift and curl in the air above the besieged village.

The Berks of Berka were a bit upset by this turn of events.

"Look, their alarm system has gone off!"

"We were told it would be out of action!"

Even so, Derek and the villagers still had a fight on their hands. They had to hold out long enough for reinforcements to arrive from the forest.

The Princess Anka grabbed an axe and waded straight in.

From what Derek could see from behind his shield, his troops seemed to be holding on. The Berks launched a last, fierce assault, but then a horn sounded from the hills... Sven Forkbeard had arrived, with the finest fighting men in the region.

The Berks were worried.
"It's a trap!"
"We're surrounded!"

It wasn't a retreat. It was a rout. The Berks cleared out, Derek cleaned up, and the Venerable Terry vanished, never to be seen again.

Sven Forkbeard slapped Derek on the shoulder.

Everyone agreed that even the real chief would have struggled to do much better than Derek had done. They seemed to think he was some kind of military genius. Unfortunately, the Vikings were a messy lot during battles, so Upper Elkshead looked very untidy again.

This time no one complained during the clean-up. Except Olaf Dednafffellur. He was beside himself with anger. Derek had given him the job of potting some plants, and he muttered curses beneath his moustache.

Chapter Seven: I Like the Reign.

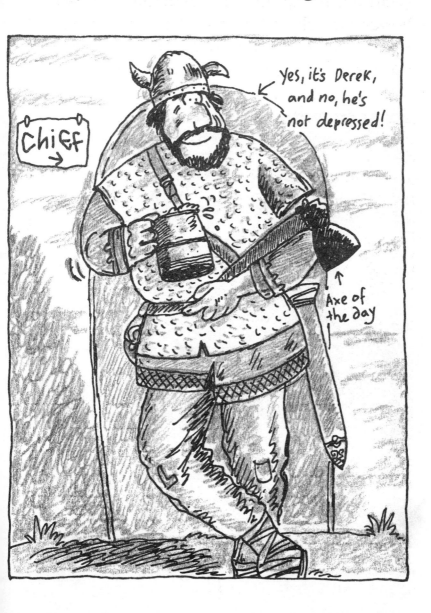

The last few days of Derek's spell in charge passed more peacefully. The treacherous Venerable Terry had gone, Olaf had run out of evil ideas, and happily everyone seemed to have forgotten about the bear-wrestling.

The only really bad thing to happen was a visit from Ethelred and Athelstane*, two antique-dealers from Holy Island, with whom Derek had once done business.

They'd started a new Chain-Mail Order Catalogue.

* See '*Who'd be a Viking?*'

It was called 'Abbey-Tat', and they wanted Derek to help them sell their wares to the Vikings of Upper Elkshead.

Ethelred and Athelstane were very good salesmen and in no time at all they'd set up shop in the village.

"I need some Athel-*stain* Remover," grumbled Derek to himself. "If we don't get rid of these two soon, we'll have spent all the Chief's gold reserves and he won't be happy!"

But try as he might, Derek couldn't think of a way to get rid of them. So imagine his delight when, one evening, just as the sun was going down beneath Princess Anka's golden hair, Derek spied a familiar silhouette in the evening sky... It was Frank, his guardian seagull, back at last from his holidays. (Gull 18-30.)

Derek recounted the story of his six-day reign – the night in the bed, the bear-wrestling, the attack by the Berks...

59

Derek explained the problems he was having with Ethelred and Athelstane. Frank hopped from foot to foot (as seagulls do when they're thinking).

"I don't think there's too much to worry about there. We just need to employ a bit of sly-chology. That's like Psy-chology, but more cunning..." And he squawked his plan into Derek's ear...

*

Ethelred and Athelstane were delighted to hear that the Berks of Berka didn't have a single shopping outlet in their village.

Frank made sure they paid lots of gold for the information and for a letter of introduction to the Venerable Terry.

"What a team!" smiled Derek, as the two monks paddled off as fast as their oars would carry them.

"Them or us?" asked Frank, perched on a post.

"Both!"

Chapter Eight: Chief at Half the Price.

Chief Harald had returned to Upper Elkshead. He looked bronzed and fit, and the first thing he did was to shake Derek's hand.

"Well done, lad. You've done a good job."

For once, Derek didn't feel too depressed.

"Now, get your stuff out of my hut and get back to your mother's." (The Chief was not a sentimental man!)

Derek's reign in charge of the village was over, and soon he was back sleeping among the goats in a corner of his mother's hut.

Frank came and stood by the door.

"I don't suppose you'll be needing me any more," he squawked, sadly. "You seem to have handled all your problems very well without me."

"Are you joking?" groaned Derek. "I've been appointed the Chief's new bear-wrestling trainer, there are two battles planned for the weekend, and the Princess Anka has been seen in the company of a good-looking swordsman from Lower Elkshead."

Frank's last page speech.

"So that's it, guys and gulls. Looks like I'll be back on the scene soon to help our man in Upper Elkshead. Stay tuned for another rune, until when keep your heads down and your shields high!"

This is Frankie S saying "BYE!"

The End